WITHDRAWN

Hello, Hedgehog! ™

Who Needs a Checkup?

Norm Feuti

ACORN ™
SCHOLASTIC INC.

For Michele —NF

All rights reserved. Published by Scholastic Inc., *Publishers since 1920.* SCHOLASTIC, ACORN, and associated logos are trademarks and/or registered trademarks of Scholastic Inc.

The publisher does not have any control over and does not assume any responsibility for author or third-party websites or their content.

Library of Congress Cataloging-in-Publication Data Available

Names: Feuti, Norman, author, illustrator.
Title: Who needs a checkup? / Norm Feuti.
Description: First edition. | New York, NY : Acorn/Scholastic Inc., 2020. |
Series: Hello, Hedgehog! ; 3 | Summary: Harry is worried about his trip to the doctor for a checkup, so his best friend Hedgehog comes up with a way to reassure him.
Identifiers: LCCN 2019013850| ISBN 9781338281446 (pbk.) | ISBN 9781338281453 (reinforced library binding)
Subjects: LCSH: Hedgehogs—Juvenile fiction. | Fear of doctors—Juvenile fiction. | Best friends—Juvenile fiction. | CYAC: Medical care—Fiction. | Hedgehogs—Fiction. | Best friends—Fiction. | Friendship—Fiction.
Classification: LCC PZ7.1.F52 Wh 2020 | DDC [E]--dc23
LC record available at https://lccn.loc.gov/2019013850

10 9 8 7 6 5 4 3 2 1   20 21 22 23 24

Printed in China   62
First edition, February 2020
Edited by Katie Carella
Book design by Maria Mercado

4

5

7

18

23

New Plans

35

Norm Feuti lives in Massachusetts with his family, a dog, two cats, and a guinea pig. He is the creator of the newspaper comic strips **Retail** and **Gil**. He is also the author and illustrator of the graphic novel **The King of Kazoo**. **Hello, Hedgehog!** is Norm's first early reader series.

YOU CAN DRAW HEDGEHOG!

1. Draw a jelly bean shape.

2. Draw the eyes, eyebrows, nose, and mouth.

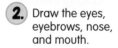

3. Add ears, lots of quills, and a doctor hat.

4. Draw little arms and legs. Draw a tiny hammer in one hand.

5. Put black spots on the ends of the quills. Draw a doctor bag.

6. Color in your drawing!

WHAT'S YOUR STORY?

Hedgehog plays checkup with Harry.
Imagine Hedgehog plays checkup with **you**.
What parts of the checkup would you like?
What parts would you not like?
Write and draw your story!